THIS BOOK
BELONGS TO:

Sarah Gowani

DATE RECEIVED: _____

Deep in the ocean, in the coral reef, among the shipwrecks and seaweed, the ocean creatures live and play. Here is what happened to them one warm and sunny day.

Peatree the parrotfish was swimming along, minding her own business, when she overheard some fish talking. "They say there's a treasure in the shipwreck on the other side of the sandbar." One fish said.

Then another answered, "Yes, they say anyone whose tried just comes back with barnacles stuck all over them. It takes a week just to remove them."

Peatree thought, "If I could get that treasure, I would be the most famous and wealthy fish in the ocean. So Peatree decided when she woke the next day, she would make the long trek to the rusty old shipwreck to collect her treasure.

As Peatree crossed the sandbar and looked down in the deep cold ocean on the other side, she thought "Gee, I've never been this far before. Maybe I should turn back." She quickly decided to continue on and worry later about getting lost.

It wasn't long after that when Peatree DID start to worry that she, in fact, was lost.

"I've been going around in circles for too long now, without any sign of the shipwreck," she said with concern. She began looking around frantically, when she saw something she'd never seen before. It was a sign that said "Shipwreck This Way."

Peatree decided it was a pretty good idea to follow the sign. She swam in the direction that the sign was pointing– past a cliff and into some dense seaweed. Then, as she swam through an especially dense patch of seaweed, she saw an opening and something enormous.

As she approached the side of the enormous boat, Peatree wondered if she should actually go inside. It was very dark in there and there might possibly be some large fish skulking around as well.

"Don't worry about that now" she said, "the treasure is too close to turn around."

On she went through the rusted belly of the giant ship. She looked side to side, forward and backward and up and down, wondering if there was anyone else in there with her. Suddenly, out of the dark, appeared a large fish. Peatree was frozen with fear.

"Peatree, what are you doing here?" asked the fish.

"Calypso the catfish, is that you?" Peatree asked.

"It's me, Calypso, at your service," he replied as he came out of the shadows. Calypso swam over and put his large fin around Peatree. He said, "You look a little lost, my friend."

"Maybe just a little," replied Peatree, "but I'll be just fine on my own, thanks."

"Suit yourself," said Calypso.
"I sure hope you find what
you're looking for." With that,
Calypso disappeared into the
darkness.

Again, Peatree found herself
alone, with no sign of the
treasure. She was just about to
give up and call out for Calypso,
when she saw something out of
the corner of her eye. It was
another sign which read:
"Treasure Through Here."